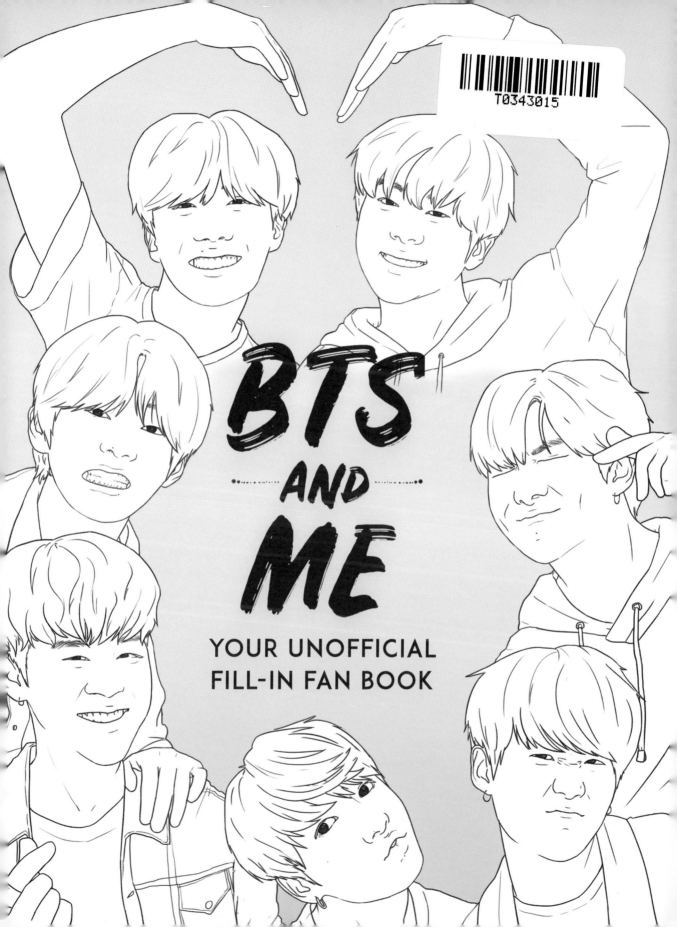

BTS

AND

ME

YOUR UNOFFICIAL
FILL-IN FAN BOOK

Written by Becca Wright

Illustrators

Salomé Robert, aka finny red, is an illustrator from France who is inspired by BTS's heartfelt lyrics and passion for their art. She can be found on Instagram @finny.red.

Ani Iashvili, aka zotte, is an illustrator from Georgia who has loved BTS's music since 2014. She can be found on Instagram @byzotte.

Line illustrations by **James Newman Gray**.

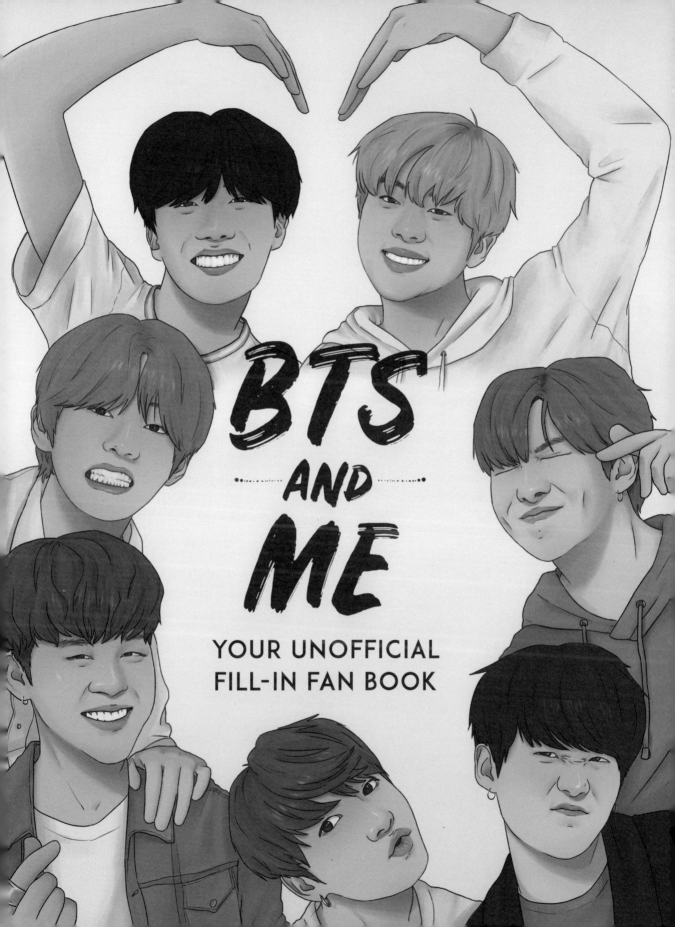

BTS
AND
ME

YOUR UNOFFICIAL
FILL-IN FAN BOOK

For Hannah

First published in Great Britain in 2019 by
Michael O'Mara Books Limited
9 Lion Yard
Tremadoc Road
London SW4 7NQ

A CIP catalogue record for this book is available from the British Library.

Papers used by Michael O'Mara Books Limited are natural, recyclable
products made from wood grown in sustainable forests. The
manufacturing processes conform to the environmental regulations of
the country of origin.

ISBN: 978-1-78929-133-9 in paperback print format

5 6 7 8 9 10

Cover design by Ana Bjezancevic
Interior design by Ana Bjezancevic and Barbara Ward
Front cover illustration by Salomé Robert
Back cover illustration by Ani Iashvili
Line illustrations by James Newman Gray
Background patterns from shutterstock.com

Printed and bound in China

Follow us on Twitter @OMaraBooks

www.mombooks.com

CONTENTS

All About Me: The Fact File 7

Bangtan Sonyeondan Timeline 8

Fact File: RM 12

A Perfect Day with RM 14

Today, My Favourite … 16

Write a Letter to Jungkook 17

Jimin's Cutest Moments 18

Draw Your Selfie 19

My Favourite Run BTS! Moments 20

My Favourite Things about J-Hope 21

Write a Letter from V to ARMY 22

Who's Your Bias? 23

My Favourite Things about Jimin 24

Write a Letter from Suga to ARMY 25

A Day Out in Seoul with BTS 26

Fact File: Jin 28

A Perfect Day with Jin 30

Who's Your BFF? Hyung Line Edition 32

Be BTS's Stylist for the Day 36

Write a Letter to J-Hope 40

Today, My Favourite … 41

My Favourite Things about V 42

Write a letter from Jimin to ARMY 43

Fact File: Suga 44

A Perfect Day with Suga 46

Slumber Party 48

Teen Movie 50

Write a Letter from Jungkook to ARMY 52

Today, My Favourite … 53

My Favourite Albums 54

Draw Your Selfie 55

Write a Letter to RM 56

My Favourite Bon Voyage Moments 57

V's Most Artistic Moments 58

My Favourite Things about Jungkook 59

Fact File: J-Hope 60

A Perfect Day with J-Hope 62

Learn to Write Hangul 64

Write a Letter from J-Hope to ARMY 68

Jungkook's Cheekiest Maknae Moments 69

On Holiday with BTS 70

The World Cup of BTS Music Videos 72

Write a Letter to Jin 74

My Favourite Things about Suga 75

Fact File: Jimin 76

A Perfect Day with Jimin 78

Jin's Worst Jokes 80

Draw Your Selfie 81

Who's Your BFF? Maknae Line Edition 82

Would You Rather ... 86

My Favourite Music Videos 88

Write a Letter to Suga 89

My Favourite Things about RM 90

Write a Letter from Jin to ARMY 91

Fact File: V 92

A Perfect Day with V 94

The World Cup of BTS Songs 96

Bangtan Firsts 98

J-Hope's Most Outrageous Fashion Choices 99

My Favourite Bangtan Bombs 100

My Favourite Things about Jin 101

Today, My Favourite ... 102

RM's Most Profound Moments 103

Next Time on Bon Voyage ... 104

Write a Letter from RM to ARMY 106

My Favourite Songs 107

Fact File: Jungkook 108

A Perfect Day with Jungkook 110

Write a Letter to V 112

My Favourite Hairstyles 113

Today, My Favourite ... 114

Suga's Most Savage Moments 115

Write a Letter to Jimin 116

My Favourite Outfits 117

Plan Your Perfect Concert 118

Design Your Perfect Concert Outfit 120

Most Likely To ... 122

Today, My Favourite ... 124

Predicting the Future 125

Audition Time 126

Glossary 128

ALL ABOUT ME: THE FACT FILE

MY NAME IS

....

MY NICKNAME IS

....

My date of birth is
_____

I was born in
_____

My star sign is
_____

My Chinese zodiac sign is
_____

I love BTS because _____
_____
_____

My parents are
_____
_____

My special talents are
_____
_____
_____
_____

BANGTAN SONYEONDAN TIMELINE

You know BTS? Just in case you don't, here's a brief timeline of some of the major dates.

2010

RM, Suga and J-Hope join Bang Si-hyuk's entertainment company, BigHit

2012

Jungkook, V, Jin and Jimin join the line-up, the name Bangtan Sonyeondan is chosen, and the first video is added to their YouTube channel

2013

11 June: First music video, for 'No More Dream', is released

12 June: BTS's debut single album, *2 Cool 4 Skool*, is released

13 June: Official debut! BTS make their mark, performing 'No More Dream' on *M Countdown*

9 July: BTS announce their official fandom name, and ARMY is born

2 September: First episode of *Rookie King* airs

11 September: *O!RUL8,2?* is released

14 November: BTS win their first award! 'Best New Artist' at the Melon Music Awards

2014

12 February: *Skool Luv Affair* is released

14 May: *Skool Luv Affair: Special Addition* is released

1 July: First episode of *American Hustle Life* airs

19 August: First full studio album, *Dark & Wild*, is released

17 October: First world tour, *The Red Bullet*, commences

2015

10 February: BTS tour Japan with *Wake Up: Open Your Eyes*

20 March: *RM*, RM's first solo mixtape, is released

29 April: *The Most Beautiful Moment in Life, Part 1* is released

1 August: First episode of *Run BTS!* airs on V Live

30 November: *The Most Beautiful Moment in Life, Part 2* is released

2016

2 May: *The Most Beautiful Moment in Life: Young Forever* is released

5 July: First season of *Bon Voyage* airs on V Live

15 August: *Agust D*, Suga's first solo mixtape, is released

10 October: *Wings* is released

2017

13 February: *You Never Walk Alone* is released

18 February: Second world tour, *Wings*, commences

21 May: BTS win 'Top Social Artist' at the Billboard Music Awards in the USA

18 September: *Love Yourself: Her* is released

19 November: BTS become the first K-pop act to perform at the American Music Awards

2018

2 March: *Hope World*, J-Hope's first solo mixtape, is released

28 March: *Burn the Stage*, a documentary following BTS on their *Wings* tour, is released on YouTube

18 May: *Love Yourself: Tear* is released

20 May: BTS win 'Top Social Artist' at the BBMAs for the second year in a row

24 August: *Love Yourself: Answer* is released

25 August: Third world tour, *Love Yourself*, commences

24 September: BTS speak at the United Nations, about their 'Love Myself' UNICEF campaign

22 October: BTS appear on the cover of *TIME* magazine

23 October: *mono.*, RM's second solo mixtape, or 'playlist', is released

24 October: BTS receive the Hwagwan Order of Cultural Merit

15 November: *Burn the Stage: The Movie* gets worldwide cinematic release

2019

26 January: *Love Yourself in Seoul*, a recording of their *Love Yourself* concert, gets worldwide cinematic release

11 February: BTS attend the Grammys in LA

12 April: *Map of the Soul: Persona* is released

1 May: BTS perform at the BBMAs, win 'Top Social Artist' for the *third* year running, and also win 'Top Duo/Group'

1–2 June: BTS play two sold-out concerts at London's Wembley Stadium

7 August: *Bring the Soul: The Movie* gets worldwide cinematic release

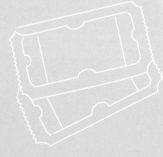

>>> FACT FILE

NAME

Kim Namjoon 김남준

ALSO KNOWN AS

Namjoonie, Rap Monster, God
of Destruction, Dance Prodigy

DATE OF BIRTH

12 September 1994

STAR SIGN

Virgo

CHINESE ZODIAC

Dog

HEIGHT

1.81m / 5'11"

BIRTHPLACE

Ilsan, South Korea

SIBLINGS

one younger sister

SKILLS

rapping, songwriting, music
production, languages,
breaking things

A PERFECT DAY
WITH RM

If you could spend *just one day* with BTS's charismatic leader RM, what would you do? Fill in the spaces below to create your own perfect day with Kim Namjoon.

Your alarm wakes you up bright and early, and you spring out of bed to get ready for what you feel is sure to be a perfect day. You shower, throw on your favourite comfortable outfit, of _____, grab some breakfast and then wait eagerly by the door.

When your doorbell rings, you open it to find Namjoon on your doorstep, holding two takeaway coffee cups. 'Here, I got you a _____, your favourite,' he says, handing you the cup.

You stroll along in the morning sunshine until you reach the river. 'Here we are,' Namjoon says, and gets out his phone, handing you an earbud, 'let's listen to music together.' You put in one earbud and he puts in the other, and you recognise the opening notes of one of your favourite songs, _____ by _____.

After a relaxing walk along the river – where you even spotted a wild _____ at the water's edge – Namjoon announces that it's time for lunch. 'Let's get _____,' he says.

At the restaurant, you order your favourite dish, _____, he orders _____, and you both get _____ to drink. It's all delicious, of course.

After a short journey out of the city, you arrive at the entrance to some kind of park. Namjoon leads you excitedly through the gate and you gasp as you see a beautiful lake, with some of your favourite animals, _____, roaming freely through the grass and trees. As you're stroking a wild _____, Namjoon asks you: '_____?' and you reply '_____.'

After spending the afternoon in the wildlife park, you head back to the city. 'This really has been a perfect day,' you sigh, as Namjoon drops you off at your front door, hugging you goodbye.

TODAY, MY FAVOURITE ...

Use this page to record what your current favourite BTS-related things are – there are several of these pages scattered throughout the book, so make sure you fill them out on different days and see how your tastes change!

Today's date: _____   Today's mood: _____

My favourite member of BTS: _____

My favourite song: _____

My favourite music video: _____

My favourite rap line song: _____

My favourite vocal line song: _____

My favourite solo song: _____

My favourite lyric: _____

My favourite dance routine: _____

My favourite Bangtan Bomb: _____

My favourite tweet: _____

WRITE A LETTER TO JUNGKOOK

Use the space below to write a letter to the Golden Maknae himself, Jungkook. You can be as silly or as heartfelt as you like – what does Jungkook mean to you? What about him inspires you? What would you say to him if he was right there in front of you?

Dear Jungkook,

Love from,

JIMIN'S CUTEST MOMENTS

Jimin is undeniably one of the cutest members of BTS, whether he's seeking praise and reassurance from his hyungs or smiling sweetly for the camera. Use the space below to list the most adorable Jimin moments.

1. _____
2. _____
3. _____
4. _____
5. _____
6. _____
7. _____
8. _____
9. _____
10. _____

DRAW YOUR SELFIE

BTS love nothing more than a good selfie, but wouldn't you like to get involved? Draw yourself into the middle of the selfie below.

And why not colour it in, too?

MY FAVOURITE RUN BTS! MOMENTS

We all love watching the boys mess about on *Run BTS!*, but what are your favourite episodes or moments from the series? Will paintballing make the cut, or are you more of a fashion show fan?

1.

2.

3.

4.

5.

6.

7.

8.

9.

10.

MY FAVOURITE THINGS ABOUT J-HOPE

You're his hope, he's your hope, he's J-Hope! The sunshine of BTS, the brilliant dancer and smooth rapper, the *aegyo* king ... the rest of Bangtan love him and so do we. Use the space below to list your favourite things about Bangtan's dance machine, Jung Hoseok.

1.

2.

3.

4.

5.

6.

7.

8.

9.

10.

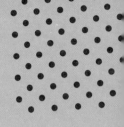

WRITE A LETTER FROM V TO ARMY

The BTS boys love telling ARMY how important they are to them – without ARMY's unwavering love and support, BTS wouldn't be where they are today. Use the space below to imagine what V might write in a letter to ARMY.

Dear ARMY,

Love from V xo

WHO'S YOUR BIAS?

Of course we love every member of BTS, but everyone's got a favourite – who's yours? And who's your bias-wrecker – that member who always looks so good or sings so well that it makes you doubt whether you picked the right bias? Use the space below to write their names, why they're your bias / bias-wrecker, and do a quick doodle of them.

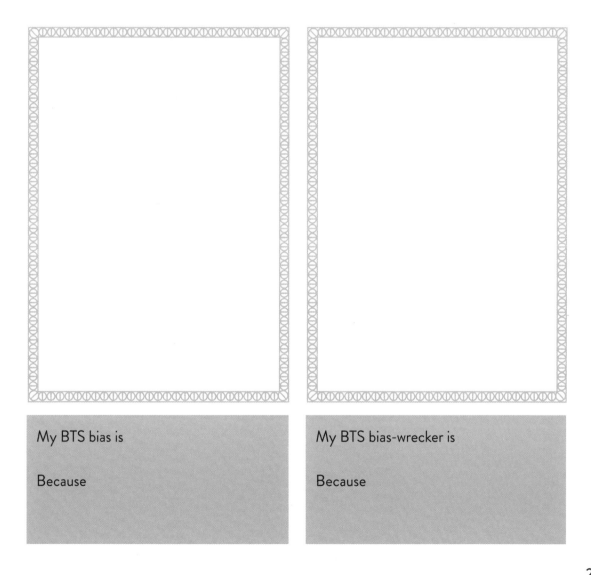

My BTS bias is

Because

My BTS bias-wrecker is

Because

MY FAVOURITE THINGS
ABOUT JIMIN

Jimin – not only has he got jams, but he's also got the voice of an angel. And the face of an angel. And the dance moves of an angel. Use the space below to list your favourite things about Bangtan's angel-in-residence, Park Jimin.

1.

2.

3.

4.

5.

6.

7.

8.

9.

10.

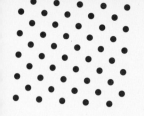

WRITE A LETTER
FROM SUGA TO ARMY

The BTS boys love telling ARMY how important they are
to them – without ARMY's unwavering love and support,
BTS wouldn't be where they are today. Use the space below
to imagine what Suga might write in a letter to ARMY.

Dear ARMY,

Love from Suga xo

A DAY OUT IN SEOUL WITH BTS

START
The limo pulls up outside your hotel. When you get in, RM asks: 'So, what do you want to do first?'

You want to see their studio, of course! Suga shows you his 'Genius Lab' and plays you a sneak preview of a new song, and then …

… you agree to pose for V as he takes some artistic portrait shots of you with his new camera.

… J-Hope offers to teach you the choreography to the new BTS single, so it's off to the dance studio!

You want to see the sights, so you wander around one of Seoul's many historic palaces, buy some souvenirs, and then …

… decide it's time for some more retail therapy; all eight of you buy matching hats and take some ridiculous selfies.

… you continue the sightseeing by helicopter, as the boys excitedly point out all of the famous landmarks.

You've won the chance to hang out with BTS for the day – what will you get up to?

... the funfair! You win a stuffed koala for RM, and Jungkook convinces you to ride the rollercoasters with him.

After helping Jin to prepare a delicious lunch for you and the boys, you decide to head off to ...

... the aquarium, where Jimin excitedly points out all of his favourite animals and you take selfies with the sea turtles.

END
After all that excitement, you finish the day with a VIP ticket to the BTS concert in Seoul – perfect!

... go to the water park and ride the log flumes and rapids until you're all completely soaked.

After stopping for a lunch of traditional Korean bibimbap, you all agree that the best way to spend the afternoon is to ...

... visit the BTS photography exhibition, where you're given a private tour by seven very handsome tour guides.

27

JIN
진

NAME
Kim Seokjin 김석진

ALSO KNOWN AS
Worldwide Handsome, Car Door
Guy, Third One From The Left

DATE OF BIRTH
4 December 1992

STAR SIGN
Sagittarius

CHINESE ZODIAC
Monkey

HEIGHT
1.79m / 5'10"

BIRTHPLACE
Gwacheon, South Korea

SIBLINGS
one older brother

SKILLS
singing, acting, cooking, making
hearts appear from nowhere,
being handsome

A PERFECT DAY
WITH JIN

If you could spend *just one day* with BTS's Worldwide Handsome vocalist Jin, what would you do? Fill in the spaces below to create your own perfect day with Kim Seokjin.

Your doorbell rings, and you open the door to find Seokjin on your doorstep, holding two freshly-baked _____. You step out the door, wearing _____ and _____, and ask: 'So, what's the plan?'

'Well, first I thought we could take a walk downtown, see the sights, maybe grab some coffee?' You agree, and as you walk arm-in-arm through the city, you ask him '_____?' He replies: '_____.'

After your walk, you grab a quick lunch of _____ before heading to the amusement arcade, where you play _____. You beat Seokjin at _____ but he wins at _____. Between the two of you, you win enough tickets to trade in for _____, which he lets you keep.

'Shall we head back to the dorm?' Seokjin asks as you leave the arcade. 'I was thinking of cooking _____ for dinner – you can help if you like!'

Seokjin does most of the cooking, but you help with _____ and

have a delicious meal.

After dinner, you head back into the city, to a karaoke bar. Seokjin starts out

strong when he sings _____ by _____

but he concedes defeat when you sing _____ by

_____. 'You should join BTS!' he jokes – you wish he was

being serious. After a few more songs each, Seokjin drops you back off at

your home and hugs you goodnight. It has been a perfect day.

WHO'S YOUR BFF?

HYUNG LINE EDITION

Take this quiz to find out which of the older boys would be your best friend – will it be Jin, RM, Suga or J-Hope?

1. What's the best way to spend a Saturday?

a. Sleeping late, eating, then sleeping some more ☐
b. Riding your bike down to the river for some quiet contemplation ☐
c. Shopping, of course! ☐
d. Trying out that new recipe you've been meaning to cook ☐

2. What's your dream job? Apart from being an idol, of course.

a. Basketball player ☐
b. Literature professor ☐
c. Choreographer ☐
d. Actor ☐

3. What's your personal style?

a. Black, black and more black ☐
b. Cool and quirky street style ☐
c. High-end fashion, baby ☐
d. Half classic and elegant, half ridiculous and dorky ☐

4. What would you get your best friend for their birthday?

a.   Expensive headphones ☐
b.   A cute cartoon figurine ☐
c.   A fun accessory that's so ugly it's cool! ☐
d.   An unusual cookbook ☐

5. How do you do your homework?

a.   You always leave it until the last minute but somehow end up with good grades anyway ☐
b.   You spend ages on it, and you always get full marks – hard work pays off! ☐
c.   Homework? You'd rather be doing anything else ... ☐
d.   You give it your best shot, but you're not too bothered about being top of the class ☐

6. What's your star skill?

a.   You're a born musician – writing songs is second nature to you, whether that's on the piano keys or the computer keys ☐
b.   You have a real way with words – poems, songs, essays, you're brilliant at them all ☐
c.   Dance is your passion, and you can nail any style you turn your mind to ☐
d.   Is being devastatingly good-looking a skill? Because if so, that's you! ☐

7. What's your favourite thing about going on holiday?

a. It's a well-earned chance to rest

b. You love exploring new places

c. It's a chance to have fun and make new memories

d. You love chatting to new people from different cultures

8. Which Korean food would you most like to try?

a. Korean BBQ

b. Kalguksu (thick noodles in hot broth)

c. Kimchi (spicy fermented cabbage)

d. Naengmyeon (cold, thin noodles in chilled broth)

9. What colour would you like to dye your hair?

a. A fresh minty green

b. A cool, shiny silver-grey

c. A bright, rich red

d. A daring bleach-blonde

10. Which of these songs is your favourite?

a. 'Trivia 轉: Seesaw'

b. 'Trivia 承: Love'

c. 'Trivia 起: Just Dance'

d. 'Epiphany'

Mostly As: Suga

You and Suga are so alike, you're sure to be firm friends. You can (and will) nap anywhere, but when you're not sneaking some shut-eye, you're working hard on your passion projects.

Mostly Bs: RM

RM is the best best friend you could ask for – you could spend hours together discussing your favourite books or taking a walk together in quiet contemplation, and you know that you'll always support each other.

Mostly Cs: J-Hope

There's never a dull moment where you and J-Hope are involved – whether you're shopping together, dancing together, or going on crazy adventures together, you'll always be having fun.

Mostly Ds: Jin

You and Jin might get mistaken for quiet, conventional types, but really, you love nothing more than to goof around, meet new people and try new things – especially if those things are edible!

BE BTS'S STYLIST FOR THE DAY

BTS are known for their unique off-duty fashion choices, intricate stage outfits and breathtaking music video aesthetics. If you could design an outfit for each member, what would you want to see them in? Use the figures on these pages to design and colour your own costume designs for the boys.

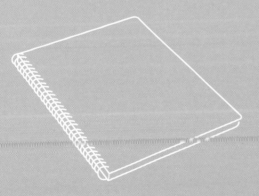

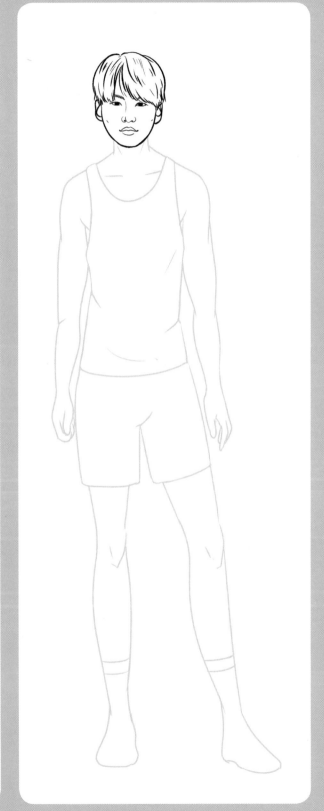

WRITE A LETTER TO J-HOPE

Use the space below to write a letter to the sunshine of BTS, J-Hope. You can be as silly or as heartfelt as you like – what does J-Hope mean to you? What about him inspires you? What would you say to him if he was right there in front of you?

Dear J-Hope,

Love from,

TODAY, MY FAVOURITE ...

Use this page to record what your current favourite
BTS-related things are – there are several of these pages
scattered throughout the book, so make sure you fill them
out on different days and see how your tastes change!

Today's date: _____   Today's mood: _____

My favourite member of BTS: _____

My favourite song: _____

My favourite music video: _____

My favourite rap line song: _____

My favourite vocal line song: _____

My favourite solo song: _____

My favourite lyric: _____

My favourite dance routine: _____

My favourite Bangtan Bomb: _____

My favourite tweet: _____

MY FAVOURITE THINGS ABOUT V

V has a silky, soulful voice, devastating dance moves, and, well, *that* face. He's a creative soul who loves to be artistic. Use the space below to write down your favourite things about Bangtan's Prince of Duality, Kim Taehyung.

1. _____
2. _____
3. _____
4. _____
5. _____
6. _____
7. _____
8. _____
9. _____
10. _____

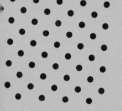

WRITE A LETTER FROM JIMIN TO ARMY

The BTS boys love telling ARMY how important they are to them – without ARMY's unwavering love and support, BTS wouldn't be where they are today. Use the space below to imagine what Jimin might write in a letter to ARMY.

Dear ARMY,

Love from Jimin xo

FACT FILE

SUGA
슈가

NAME

Min Yoongi 민윤기

ALSO KNOWN AS

Agust D, Gloss, Motionless
Min, 'Min Suga – Genius'

DATE OF BIRTH

9 March 1993

STAR SIGN

Pisces

CHINESE ZODIAC

Rooster

HEIGHT

1.74m / 5'9"

BIRTHPLACE

Daegu, South Korea

SIBLINGS

one older brother

SKILLS

rapping, songwriting,
music production, playing
piano, napping

A PERFECT DAY
WITH SUGA

If you could spend *just one day* with BTS's rapper (and napper) extraordinaire, what would you do? Fill in the spaces below to create your own perfect day with Min Yoongi.

Your day starts with a nice long lie-in – you're sure Yoongi will be doing the same. After a leisurely start, your doorbell rings mid-morning and you open it to find a sleepy-looking Yoongi on your doorstep, clutching two cups of _____, with his dog, Holly, next to him.

'Good morning _____,' he says, handing you one of the cups, 'I've got a special plan for today – I want to adopt a friend for Holly.' You love his dog almost as much as he does, and you squeal in excitement.

You arrive at the dog shelter and start looking around at all the rescued dogs – all different breeds, some of them bounding up to greet you, Yoongi and Holly, some of them shy and nervous. 'What about that one?' you say, pointing to a _____. Yoongi approaches and the dog comes over to nuzzle his hand, before sniffing cautiously at Holly. Before long though, the two dogs are playing with each other and yapping excitedly. 'Perfect!' he beams, reading the name on the collar. 'I think _____ and Holly will be great friends.'

You leave the dog shelter with two dogs in tow, and grab a quick lunch of _____ from a street vendor, which you eat as you wander through the park, Holly getting to know his new friend. '_____?' you ask, and Yoongi replies: '_____.'

After an afternoon walk in the park with Yoongi and the dogs, you head back to Yoongi's flat, flop down on the sofa and order _____ for dinner – you choose _____ and Yoongi picks _____.

'So, what shall we watch?' he asks, handing you the remote. You pick _____ and settle in for a cozy night on the sofa with Yoongi, Holly, _____ and a good film; a perfect end to a perfect day.

SLUMBER PARTY

The boys work so hard on their singing, rapping and dancing – don't you think they deserve a break? Colour them in and think about what they'd need for the perfect sleepover.

TEEN MOVIE

Imagine you were casting the boys in a high school movie – who would you cast in each role, and why?

THE JOCK
THE NERD
THE PREP
THE CHEERLEADER
THE SKATER
THE GOTH
THE BAD BOY

Role:

Because:

Role:

Because:

Role:

Because:

Role:

Because:

Role:

Because:

Role:

Because:

Role:

Because:

WRITE A LETTER
FROM JUNGKOOK TO ARMY

The BTS boys love telling ARMY how important they are to them – without ARMY's unwavering love and support, BTS wouldn't be where they are today. Use the space below to imagine what Jungkook might write in a letter to ARMY.

Dear ARMY,

Love from Jungkook xo

TODAY, MY FAVOURITE ...

Use this page to record what your current favourite
BTS-related things are – there are several of these pages
scattered throughout the book, so make sure you fill them
out on different days and see how your tastes change!

Today's date: _____   Today's mood: _____

My favourite member of BTS: _____

My favourite song: _____

My favourite music video: _____

My favourite rap line song: _____

My favourite vocal line song: _____

My favourite solo song: _____

My favourite lyric: _____

My favourite dance routine: _____

My favourite Bangtan Bomb: _____

My favourite tweet: _____

MY FAVOURITE ALBUMS

BTS have been releasing music since 2013 – and we love it all, of course. But if you *had* to rank them, which album takes the top spot?

1.
2.
3.
4.
5.
6.
7.
8.
9.
10.
11.
12.
13.

» *2 Cool 4 Skool*

» *O!RUL8,2?*

» *Skool Luv Affair*

» *Dark & Wild*

» *The Most Beautiful Moment in Life, Part 1*

» *The Most Beautiful Moment in Life, Part 2*

» *The Most Beautiful Moment in Life: Young Forever*

» *Wings*

» *You Never Walk Alone*

» *Love Yourself: Her*

» *Love Yourself: Tear*

» *Love Yourself: Answer*

» *Map of the Soul: Persona*

DRAW YOUR SELFIE

BTS love nothing more than a good selfie, but wouldn't you like to get involved? Draw yourself into the middle of the selfie below.

And why not colour it in, too?

WRITE A LETTER TO RM

Use the space below to write a letter to the thoughtful leader of BTS, RM. You can be as silly or as heartfelt as you like – what does RM mean to you? What about him inspires you? What would you say to him if he was right there in front of you?

Dear RM,

Love from,

MY FAVOURITE
BON VOYAGE MOMENTS

We all love watching the boys go on holiday together, exploring new places and somehow always losing their stuff. From stargazing in Hawaii to boat rides in Scandinavia to horse riding in Malta, they've made a lot of happy memories – which are your favourites?

1. _____

2. _____

3. _____

4. _____

5. _____

6. _____

7. _____

8. _____

9. _____

10. _____

V'S MOST ARTISTIC MOMENTS

V is well-known for his artistic side, whether it's making sure he visits the art galleries in whichever city he's in or customizing his own clothes. V loves art, and we love how much he loves it. Use the space below to record your favourite artistic moments.

1. _____
2. _____
3. _____
4. _____
5. _____
6. _____
7. _____
8. _____
9. _____
10. _____

MY FAVOURITE THINGS ABOUT JUNGKOOK

Is there anything Jungkook can't do? The youngest member of BTS is an expert dancer with an incredible voice – and he's not bad at rapping, either! Use the space below to write down your favourite things about Bangtan's Golden Maknae, Jeon Jungkook.

1. _____

2. _____

3. _____

4. _____

5. _____

6. _____

7. _____

8. _____

9. _____

10. _____

J-HOPE
제이홉

NAME
Jung Hoseok 정호석

ALSO KNOWN AS
Hobi, Hope, J-Dope, Smile
Hoya, 'The Sunshine of BTS'

DATE OF BIRTH
18 February 1994

STAR SIGN
Aquarius

CHINESE ZODIAC
Dog

HEIGHT
1.77m / 5'10"

BIRTHPLACE
Gwangju, South Korea

SIBLINGS
one older sister

SKILLS
rapping, dancing, singing,
songwriting, *aegyo*, being
a ray of sunshine

A PERFECT DAY
WITH J-HOPE

If you could spend *just one day* with BTS's resident ray
of sunshine, what would you do? Fill in the spaces below
to create your own perfect day with Jung Hoseok.

'Good morning _____!' Hoseok's cheerful voice greets you as you pick

up your phone. 'Meet me outside in an hour? Oh, and pack some gym clothes.'

You jump out of bed and make yourself ready, then head downstairs to find

Hoseok parked outside, waving to you from the driver's seat.

You jump into the passenger seat and see that there are two freshly-made

smoothies in the cup-holders. 'Take one!' Hoseok says. 'We're going shopping,'

he grins. You grab a smoothie and take a sip – it's _____, your

favourite.

You spend the morning visiting all of Hoseok's favourite designer shops, where

he buys himself _____ and _____, and you choose

_____ and _____ – he pays, of course!

After that, you head to a bookshop, and he asks you what your favourite

book is, because he needs something new to read. You tell him that it's

_____ by _____ and he picks up a copy.

After grabbing a quick lunch, you hop back into Hoseok's car and he drives to the BigHit studio. 'I hope you brought those gym clothes!' he says brightly. 'I'm going to teach you the choreography for _____ – I remember you saying that was your favourite BTS song.'

After an exhausting but incredibly fun afternoon, you shower and change for dinner. Hoseok drives you to a very fancy restaurant; as you sit down, he says: 'Order whatever you like – it's on me.' You decide to try something new, and order _____, with some _____ to drink. After a long and delicious meal, he drives you home, dropping you off outside your front door. 'Thanks – I've had a perfect day!' you say, hugging him goodbye.

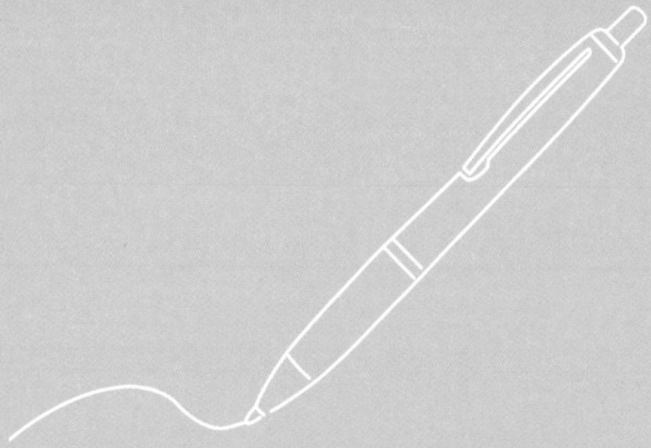

LEARN TO WRITE HANGUL

BANGTAN SONYEONDAN

방탄소년단

방탄소년단

SARANGHAE (I LOVE YOU)

사랑해

사랑해

ARMY

아미

아미

KIM NAMJOON

김남준

김남준

KIM SEOKJIN

김석진

김석진

If you've ever wondered how to write the Bangtan Boys' names in their native alphabet, now is the time to learn! Use the space on these pages to practise until your Hangul characters are perfect.

MIN YOONGI

민윤기

민윤기

JUNG HOSEOK

정호석

정호석

PARK JIMIN

박지민

박지민

KIM TAEHYUNG

김태형

김태형

JEON JUNGKOOK

전정국

전정국

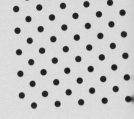

WRITE A LETTER FROM J-HOPE TO ARMY

The BTS boys love telling ARMY how important they are
to them – without ARMY's unwavering love and support,
BTS wouldn't be where they are today. Use the space below
to imagine what J-Hope might write in a letter to ARMY.

Dear ARMY,

Love from J-Hope xo

JUNGKOOK'S CHEEKIEST MAKNAE MOMENTS

As the youngest member of BTS, Jungkook ought to show his hyungs a little respect – but he's so charming that he often gets away with being pretty cheeky. Use the space below to record your favourites.

1.

2.

3.

4.

5.

6.

7.

8.

9.

10.

ON HOLIDAY WITH BTS

START

Lucky you – you're going on holiday with BTS, and you even get to pick the location. Where are you going?

To the Caribbean! As soon as you arrive you collapse into a hammock to relax as RM excitedly shows you crabs from the lagoon. Then ...

... time for a snorkelling trip! You and Jimin make friends with all the fish, but Jin doesn't seem quite as keen.

... spa treatments! Suga definitely falls asleep during his massage and J-Hope keeps making silly faces with his mud pack on.

To Canada! As soon as you're off the plane you're onto the slopes for some snowboarding with Suga and Jungkook, before ...

... you try out the sauna with J-Hope – but stepping outside into the snow afterwards is quite a shock!

... you take a husky-drawn sled out into the wilderness with V and Jimin – and some flasks of hot chocolate, of course.

You've won the chance to go on holiday with BTS – what adventures will you have?

The next day, after a lazy morning and a delicious lunch of Caribbean curry, you decide to ...

... take a trip to the local bird sanctuary, where V takes loads of pictures of the birds of paradise – and you.

... persuade Jungkook to take you on a scenic drive around the island, singing along in the car to all of your favourite songs.

After an evening of cooking over the campfire and gazing up at the stars, you get some well-earned rest, because the next day ...

... you go hiking up in the snowy mountain forests with Jin, where you spot wild deer and even a moose!

... you go kayaking down the river with RM, and catch sight of a bear fishing for salmon in the shallows.

END
Time to go, but you've got loads of photos and even more memories – this is one trip you'll never forget.

THE WORLD CUP OF BTS MUSIC VIDEOS

DNA

Boy Meets Evil

Serendipity

Danger

Fire

Forever Rain

No More Dream

Airplane

Give It To Me

Epiphany

IDOL

Dope

MIC Drop

Run

Singularity

N.O

Below are 32 BTS music videos (including some solo projects) arranged in pairs – pick your favourite from each pair as you play them off against each other until you have one left: your absolute favourite BTS music video. Which one will win?

Boy in Luv

Do You

Blood, Sweat & Tears

I Need U

Boy With Luv

Not Today

Agust D

War of Hormone

Euphoria

We Are Bulletproof pt. 2

Daydream

FAKE LOVE

Just One Day

Airplane pt. 2

Save Me

Spring Day

WRITE A LETTER
TO JIN

Use the space below to write a letter to Mr Worldwide Handsome himself, Jin. You can be as silly or as heartfelt as you like – what does Jin mean to you? What about him inspires you? What would you say to him if he was right there in front of you?

Dear Jin,

Love from,

MY FAVOURITE THINGS ABOUT SUGA

Suga might seem serious – even grumpy – at first, but as his bandmates would tell you, once you get to know him, he's a real sweetie. Use the space below to write down your favourite things about Bangtan's thoughtful rapper, Min Yoongi.

1.
2.
3.
4.
5.
6.
7.
8.
9.
10.

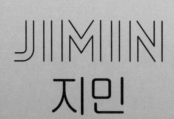

JIMIN
지민

NAME
Park Jimin 박지민

ALSO KNOWN AS
Chim Chim, Jiminie, Mochi,
Ddochi

DATE OF BIRTH
13 October 1995

STAR SIGN
Libra

CHINESE ZODIAC
Pig

HEIGHT
1.73m / 5'8"

BIRTHPLACE
Busan, South Korea

SIBLINGS
one younger brother

SKILLS
dancing, singing, taekwondo,
kendo, football, being
adorable

A PERFECT DAY
WITH JIMIN

If you could spend *just one day* with BTS's very own mochi, what would you do? Fill in the spaces below to create your own perfect day with Park Jimin.

You hear a knock on your door just as you finish getting ready, and open it to find Jimin on your doorstep, smiling and holding a bouquet of _____.

'Hey _____! I hope you're ready for brunch!' he says, 'But I guess you'd better put the flowers inside.' You put them in a vase in your living room, and then follow Jimin to the brunch place he's chosen.

'Hey, why don't we order for each other?' he suggests, as you sit down, so you order _____ and _____ for Jimin and he orders _____ and _____ for you.

After brunch, feeling full and happy, Jimin takes your hand and you follow him up to the roof of a nearby skyscraper. You gasp when you see the helicopter waiting for you. 'It's the quickest way to get to the beach!' Jimin explains.

The helicopter ride from the city to the coast is breathtaking, with Jimin beside you excitedly pointing _____ out to you. You touch down by the sea and jump down onto the soft white sand. As you walk along the beautiful

shoreline, you spot a wild _____ and quickly snap a picture, before turning your camera to Jimin, who poses cutely at the water's edge.

You spend hours at the beach, splashing around and taking photos. Then Jimin starts walking back to the helicopter; you follow, assuming it's time to head back to the city, but instead, he returns with a picnic basket and a blanket which he spreads on the sand, before unpacking all kinds of food: _____, _____, _____ and even _____! You sit side by side, enjoying the view and the food, until the sun eventually sets over the ocean.

'Well, I guess it's time to head back home, _____,' he says, and you sigh with contentment, thinking about how perfect the day has been.

JIN'S WORST JOKES

As the oldest member of BTS, Jin delights in winding up the others with his ... *unique* sense of humour. He's always making terrible jokes or pulling ridiculous faces. Use the space below to record your favourites.

1. _____
2. _____
3. _____
4. _____
5. _____
6. _____
7. _____
8. _____
9. _____
10. _____

DRAW YOUR SELFIE

BTS love nothing more than a good selfie, but wouldn't you like to get involved? Draw yourself into the middle of the selfie below.

And why not colour it in, too?

WHO'S YOUR BFF?

MAKNAE LINE EDITION

Take this quiz to find out which of the younger boys would be your best friend – will it be Jimin, V or Jungkook?

1. What's the best way to spend a Saturday?

a. Just chilling out and playing videogames ☐

b. Reading comics and listening to happy music ☐

c. Visiting an art gallery ☐

2. What's your dream job? Apart from being an idol, of course.

a. An athlete ☐

b. A police officer ☐

c. An artist ☐

3. What's your personal style?

a. You're always comfy in oversized t-shirts and big boots ☐

b. Classic stripes and a pair of colourful trainers ☐

c. Anything a bit off-beat or unusual ☐

4. What would you get your best friend for their birthday?

a. A sketchpad and some colouring pencils ☐

b. A cool hat ☐

c. A one-of-a-kind painting as unique as they are ☐

5. How do you do your homework?

a. You usually charm one of your smarter friends into letting you copy theirs ☐

b. It's always on time and you always work hard on it – you take pride in doing your absolute best ☐

c. If you're being honest, sometimes you forget about it entirely – but when you remember to do it, you're surprisingly smart ☐

6. What's your star skill?

a. You've never met a skill you couldn't master – singing, dancing, martial arts, photography, art ... you're truly multitalented ☐

b. Being absolutely adorable ☐

c. Photography – you've got a real eye for composition and detail ☐

7. What's your favourite thing about going on holiday?

a. All the different kinds of food you'll get to eat ☐

b. Doing all the fun stuff tourists get to do ☐

c. Letting yourself get totally lost and having adventures ☐

8. Which Korean food would you most like to try?

a. Dwaeji gukbap (pork rice soup) ☐

b. Kimchi jjigae (spicy kimchi and tofu stew) ☐

c. Japchae (stir-fried sweet potato noodles) ☐

9. What colour would you like to dye your hair?

a. A fun cherry red ☐

b. A cute candyfloss pink ☐

c. An eye-catching bright blue ☐

10. Which of these songs is your favourite?

a. 'Euphoria' ☐

b. 'Serendipity' ☐

c. 'Singularity' ☐

Mostly As: Jungkook

You and Jungkook are as mischievous as each other. You value your creature comforts, and like nothing more than chilling out with comfy clothes and tasty food, but you're both creatives at heart – when you get bored of videogames, you can help Jungkook with his video editing, or draw each other's portraits.

Mostly Bs: Jimin

Sweet and caring, you and Jimin are perfectly matched. Whether you're taking a tour of a new city or staying at home reading each other's favourite comics, you know you'll always have fun with each other.

Mostly Cs: V

You and V are both free spirits – some people might think you're weird, but you just know you're different. From taking photos of each other posing in art galleries to customizing each other's clothes, you'll always be up to something fun and unexpected with V.

WOULD YOU RATHER ...

These might just be the hardest choices you'll ever have to make!

cook with Jin **or**

go for a picnic with Jungkook

learn choreography with J-Hope **or**

write a song with RM

act in a scene with V **or**

make a film with Jungkook

cuddle a cat with Jimin **or**

play with a puppy with V

nap with Suga **or**

play videogames with Jungkook

explore a new city with Jimin **or**

take a tour of Seoul with RM

learn guitar with Jin **or**

learn piano with Suga

watch fireworks with Jimin **or**
paint something with Jungkook

hold a snake with J-Hope **or**
stroke a stingray with Jin

go fishing with Suga **or**
go shopping with J-Hope

go snorkelling with RM **or**
go jetskiing with Jin

go horseriding with V **or**
go hiking with RM

sing a duet with Jimin **or**
do a rap battle with Suga

visit an art gallery with V **or**
design clothes with J-Hope

MY FAVOURITE MUSIC VIDEOS

Every BTS music video is a mini-masterpiece, but which are your favourites? Are you a fan of the bright 80s visuals of 'DNA', or do you prefer the velvet decadence of 'Blood, Sweat & Tears'?

1.

2.

3.

4.

5.

6.

7.

8.

9.

10.

WRITE A LETTER TO SUGA

Use the space below to write a letter to the thoughtful and talented rapper and producer Suga. You can be as silly or as heartfelt as you like – what does Suga mean to you? What about him inspires you? What would you say to him if he was right there in front of you?

Dear Suga,

Love from,

MY FAVOURITE THINGS ABOUT RM

The brains of BTS, RM's intelligence shines through in his lyrics, and he's always looking out for his bandmates and encouraging ARMY to love themselves for who they are. Use the space below to write down your favourite things about Bangtan's charismatic leader, Kim Namjoon.

1.

2.

3.

4.

5.

6.

7.

8.

9.

10.

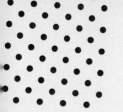

WRITE A LETTER FROM JIN TO ARMY

The BTS boys love telling ARMY how important they are to them – without ARMY's unwavering love and support, BTS wouldn't be where they are today. Use the space below to imagine what Jin might write in a letter to ARMY.

Dear ARMY,

Love Jin xo

NAME
Kim Taehyung 김태형

ALSO KNOWN AS
TaeTae, Gucci Prince, Vante

DATE OF BIRTH
30 December 1995

STAR SIGN
Capricorn

CHINESE ZODIAC
Pig

HEIGHT
1.79m / 5'10"

BIRTHPLACE
Daegu, South Korea

SIBLINGS
a younger sister and
a younger brother

SKILLS
singing, dancing, acting,
photography, getting lost

A PERFECT DAY
WITH V

If you could spend *just one day* with BTS's honey-voiced vocalist V, what would you do? Fill in the spaces below to create your own perfect day with Kim Taehyung.

You wake up to a text message from Taehyung: 'Meet me outside in an hour!' You get up and dressed, and leave your apartment to find Taehyung outside, leaning against a bicycle, camera slung around his neck, holding two freshly-baked _____.

'Hey _____!' he greets you, 'I thought we could go for a ride around the city and take some photographs!' You gratefully take the food, and gasp as you spot Yeontan, Taehyung's dog, in the basket on the front of his bike.

You set off on a leisurely bike ride through the city, stopping every so often for you and Taehyung to take turns photographing each other – and Yeontan – in front of interesting-looking buildings and graffiti. After a shot of Taehyung in front of _____ that you were particularly proud of, you suggest grabbing some lunch. You decide on _____ from a street vendor, and happily keep cycling until you reach the art gallery.

You take a couple of arty shots outside the gallery, and then wander in with Taehyung, who leads you around excitedly by the hand, showing you all of his

favourite paintings and posing in front of them. You take

him to see your favourite, too, _____.

After spending the afternoon in the art gallery, you get back on your bicycles

and follow Taehyung to a restaurant, where you are ushered inside and sit

down in a plush velvet booth. 'It's one of the best restaurants in the city,'

Taehyung says proudly, and he's not wrong. You eat _____

and he has _____, and for dessert you both order

_____.

Then you cycle lazily home, and before you step inside, you hug Taehyung

goodbye and thank him for what has been a truly perfect day.

THE WORLD CUP
OF BTS SONGS

FAKE LOVE

2! 3!

I Need U

Danger

Converse High

I'm Fine

21st Century Girl

Cypher pt. 3

Blood, Sweat & Tears

War of Hormone

Spring Day

Baepsae

Anpanman

Not Today

Fire

Cypher pt. 1

Below are 32 BTS songs arranged in pairs – pick your favourite from each pair as you play them off against each other until you have one left: your absolute favourite BTS song. Which one will win?

DNA

Airplane pt. 2

Boy With Luv

No More Dream

Save Me

Ddaeng

IDOL

24/7=Heaven

Just One Day

Boy in Luv

N.O

Tear

Pied Piper

Dope

MIC Drop

Run

BANGTAN FIRSTS

Use the space below to record all your BTS firsts – if you can still remember them!

The first song I heard:

The first music video I watched:

The first album I bought:

The first concert I went to:

The first live performance I watched:

The first member I biased:

The first Bangtan Bomb I watched:

The first dance routine I learned:

The first piece of merch I bought:

J-HOPE'S MOST OUTRAGEOUS FASHION CHOICES

J-Hope is known for his love of out-there clothing and accessories, from his chunky Balenciaga trainers to the infamous fluffy 'acorn' pouch. Use the space below to record your favourites.

1. _____

2. _____

3. _____

4. _____

5. _____

6. _____

7. _____

8. _____

9. _____

10. _____

MY FAVOURITE BANGTAN BOMBS

These short videos released on BigHit's YouTube channel are always an amusing insight into BTS's daily life, featuring everything from 'Jimin, you got no jams!' to the iconic SOPE-ME vocal duet. Use the space below to list your favourites.

1.

2.

3.

4.

5.

6.

7.

8.

9.

10.

MY FAVOURITE THINGS ABOUT JIN

More than just a pretty face, the oldest member of BTS looks out for the others, and is always trying to make them laugh. Use the space below to write down your favourite things about Bangtan's Worldwide Handsome hyung, Kim Seokjin.

1. _____
2. _____
3. _____
4. _____
5. _____
6. _____
7. _____
8. _____
9. _____
10. _____

TODAY, MY FAVOURITE ...

Use this page to record what your current favourite BTS-related things are — there are several of these pages scattered throughout the book, so make sure you fill them out on different days and see how your tastes change!

Today's date: _____   Today's mood: _____

My favourite member of BTS: _____

My favourite song: _____

My favourite music video: _____

My favourite rap line song: _____

My favourite vocal line song: _____

My favourite solo song: _____

My favourite lyric: _____

My favourite dance routine: _____

My favourite Bangtan Bomb: _____

My favourite tweet:

RM'S MOST PROFOUND MOMENTS

RM is a bit of a philosopher, and he often comes out with poetic and profound ideas about life. Use the space below to record your favourites.

1. _____
2. _____
3. _____
4. _____
5. _____
6. _____
7. _____
8. _____
9. _____
10. _____

NEXT TIME ON BON VOYAGE ...

LOCATION:

Who would you put in each room?

Room 1:

Room 2:

Room 3:

Who would you pair up for friendship trips?

Trip 1:

Trip 2:

Trip 3:

They've been to Scandinavia, Hawaii and Malta, but where would you send BTS next? Use the space below to plan the next series of *Bon Voyage*.

What activities would you plan for them?

Day 1:

Day 2:

Day 3:

Day 4:

Day 5:

Day 6:

Day 7:

Day 8:

Day 9:

Day 10:

WRITE A LETTER FROM RM TO ARMY

The BTS boys love telling ARMY how important they are to them – without ARMY's unwavering love and support, BTS wouldn't be where they are today. Use the space below to imagine what RM might write in a letter to ARMY.

Dear ARMY,

Love from RM xo

MY FAVOURITE SONGS

It's not going to be easy, but use the space below to list your absolute favourite BTS songs. If you want to make it even trickier, you can throw in their solo stuff, too.

1. _____

2. _____

3. _____

4. _____

5. _____

6. _____

7. _____

8. _____

9. _____

10. _____

JUNGKOOK
정국

NAME
Jeon Jungkook 전정국

ALSO KNOWN AS
JK, Kookie, Bunny, Nochu,
Golden Maknae

DATE OF BIRTH
1 September 1997

STAR SIGN
Virgo

CHINESE ZODIAC
Ox

HEIGHT
1.78m / 5'10"

BIRTHPLACE
Busan, South Korea

SIBLINGS
one older brother

SKILLS
singing, dancing, video
editing, videogames,
photography, drawing,
taekwondo, eating

A PERFECT DAY
WITH JUNGKOOK

If you could spend *just one day* with BTS's Golden Maknae, Jungkook, what would you do? Fill in the spaces below to create your own perfect day with Jeon Jungkook.

Your phone wakes you up with a reminder that today you're spending the day with Jungkook, so you get up and make yourself ready. The doorbell rings and you open the door to find Jungkook outside with a bright smile on his face, leaning against a car and holding two cups of _____ and two fresh _____ for breakfast.

You get in the passenger seat and Jungkook drives you to the fairground that's in town. First, you go on the _____, and then the _____, before Jungkook convinces you to go for a ride on _____. 'Don't be scared,' he says, 'I'll hold your hand!' Then Jungkook gets a new high score on the basketball hoops and wins you a _____.

You get some lunch at the fair – you get _____ and Jungkook gets _____, as well as some candyfloss for you to share. After a few more rides, Jungkook suggests you head back to his for a videogame tournament.

You settle on the sofa and Jungkook hands you a controller. 'So, what do you want to play first?' he asks; you decide on _____. It's a close

match, but you win in the end, and Jungkook tries not to sulk. 'Okay well we're playing _____ next – I'll definitely beat you at that!'

After that, you decide to order food. 'Let's get _____,' you suggest. After you finish eating, Jungkook gets your coat, and you assume he's walking you home, until he veers off down towards the river; a few minutes later, the night sky is lit up by an incredible firework display. 'I thought you'd like it,' Jungkook says shyly, putting his arm through yours.

When the fireworks are finished, Jungkook really does walk you home, hugging you goodbye as you thank him for a perfect day.

WRITE A LETTER TO V

Use the space below to write a letter to the artistic free spirit V. You can be as silly or as heartfelt as you like – what does V mean to you? What about him inspires you? What would you say to him if he was right there in front of you?

Dear V,

Love from,

MY FAVOURITE HAIRSTYLES

Since they debuted in 2013, each member of BTS has sported a dazzling array of different hair colours and styles – but which is your favourite for each member? List them below.

RM: _____

Jin: _____

Suga: _____

J-Hope: _____

Jimin: _____

V: _____

Jungkook: _____

TODAY, MY FAVOURITE ...

Use this page to record what your current favourite
BTS-related things are – there are several of these pages
scattered throughout the book, so make sure you fill them
out on different days and see how your tastes change!

Today's date: _____   Today's mood: _____

My favourite member of BTS: _____

My favourite song: _____

My favourite music video: _____

My favourite rap line song: _____

My favourite vocal line song: _____

My favourite solo song: _____

My favourite lyric: _____

My favourite dance routine: _____

My favourite Bangtan Bomb: _____

My favourite tweet: _____

SUGA'S MOST SAVAGE MOMENTS

Suga might secretly be a sweetheart, but he's got a sharp tongue and he's not afraid to use it for a withering put-down. Use the space below to record your favourites.

1.
2.
3.
4.
5.
6.
7.
8.
9.
10.

WRITE A LETTER
TO JIMIN

Use the space below to write a letter to the angel-faced and angel-voiced Jimin. You can be as silly or as heartfelt as you like – what does Jimin mean to you? What about him inspires you? What would you say to him if he was right there in front of you?

Dear Jimin,

Love from,

MY FAVOURITE OUTFITS

Each member has worn some pretty iconic clothing in the years since debut, but which is your number one look for each member? It could be a costume from a music video, a live performance or an off-duty outfit. List them below.

RM: _____

Jin: _____

Suga: _____

J-Hope: _____

Jimin: _____

V: _____

Jungkook: _____

PLAN YOUR PERFECT CONCERT

BTS are planning a very special concert in *your* city, and they need your help planning the setlist! Which songs do you most want to see the boys perform? Who do you want to star in each of the video intermissions? Will you include a mash-up, and if so, which songs do you think would work well together?

You'll have a front-row ticket, of course.

1. _____

2. _____

3. _____

4. _____

VIDEO INTERMISSION: _____

5. _____

6. _____

7. _____

8. _____

VIDEO INTERMISSION: _____

9. _____

10. _____

11. _____

12. _____

13. _____

VIDEO INTERMISSION: _____

14. _____

15. _____

16. _____

17. _____

18. _____

19. _____

20. _____

VIDEO INTERMISSION: _____

ENCORE

21. _____

ENDING SPEECHES – try not to cry as the boys thank the crowd for such a great show!

22. _____

23. _____

DESIGN YOUR PERFECT CONCERT OUTFIT

Now that you've planned your perfect Bangtan setlist, it's time to plan your outfit for the big night ...

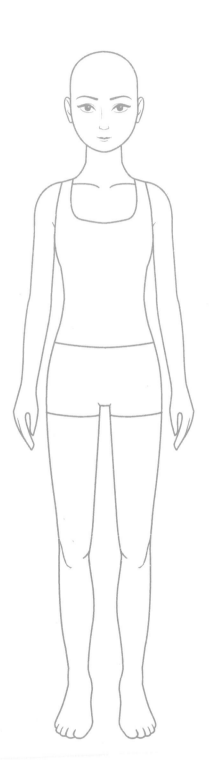

... and don't forget your best friend's outfit too!

MOST LIKELY TO ...

If the boys were no longer in BTS, which of them do you think would be most likely to do the following things?

GO TO SPACE
WRITE A BOOK
SHAVE THEIR HEAD
RUN A MARATHON
BECOME PRESIDENT
BUY A MOTORBIKE
CLIMB MOUNT EVEREST

Most likely to:

Because:

Most likely to:

Because:

Most likely to:

Because:

Most likely to:

Because:

Most likely to:

Because:

Most likely to:

Because:

Most likely to:

Because:

TODAY, MY FAVOURITE ...

Use this page to record what your current favourite BTS-related things are – there are several of these pages scattered throughout the book, so make sure you fill them out on different days and see how your tastes change!

Today's date: _____   Today's mood: _____

My favourite member of BTS: _____

My favourite song: _____

My favourite music video: _____

My favourite rap line song: _____

My favourite vocal line song: _____

My favourite solo song: _____

My favourite lyric: _____

My favourite dance routine: _____

My favourite Bangtan Bomb: _____

My favourite tweet: _____

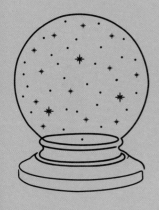

PREDICTING THE FUTURE

BTS have achieved some amazing things since they debuted in 2013, but what do you see in their future? It's time to consult your crystal ball and write down your predictions.

In the next five years, I think BTS will:

1. _____

_____

2. _____

_____

3. _____

_____

4. _____

_____

5. _____

_____

AUDITION TIME

Have you got what it takes to become the eighth member of BTS? It's your lucky day – BTS are looking for an eighth member, and it could be you! Use the space below to make your case.

First things first –
what are you wearing to your audition?

Are you auditioning as a vocalist or a rapper?
It's time to choose:

You'd better show off your skills –
which BTS song will you perform?

You have to pick one of the members to duet with – who, and what song will you pick?

Vocal skills aren't enough, though –
which dance will you perform?

Lastly, why do you think you should be the eighth member of BTS?
What sets you apart?
What makes you think you'd fit in with the boys?

GLOSSARY

AEGYO: performative cuteness, through facial expressions and body language

ARMY: the name for BTS fans – it stands for 'Adorable Representative MC for Youth'

BANGTAN BOMBS: short videos uploaded to the official YouTube channel, showing the boys messing around, preparing for shows or performing

HYUNG: a mark of respect used by men to older close male friends or brothers: for example, if being respectful, all members of BTS should address Jin as 'Jin-hyung', or 'hyung', as he is the oldest

HYUNG LINE: the four oldest members, Jin, Suga, J-Hope and RM

MAKNAE: the youngest member – in BTS, that's Jungkook

MAKNAE LINE: the three youngest members, Jimin, V and Jungkook

RAP LINE: the three rappers, RM, Suga and J-Hope

VOCAL LINE: the four vocalists, Jin, Jimin, V and Jungkook